"Hi, Pizza Man!"

by VIRGINIA WALTER
pictures by PONDER GOEMBEL

SCHOLASTIC INC.

New York Toronto London Auckland Sydney
Mexico City New Delhi Hong Kong

"Mama!"

"I'm HUNGRY!"

4

"I know you're hungry, Vivian.
It's so hard to wait
for the pizza man to come.
He'll be here soon."

"What will you say when the doorbell rings
and we open the door?"

"What if it's not a pizza man?
What if it's a pizza woman?
Then what will you say?"

"Hi, Pizza Woman!"

"What if it's not a pizza woman? What if it's a pizza kitty?
Then what will you say?"

"MEOW MEOW, PIZZA KITTY!"

"What if it's a pizza dog? Then what will you say?"

"WOOF WOOF, PIZZA DOG!"

"What if it's a pizza duck? Then what will you say?"

"QUACK QUACK, PIZZA DUCK!"

"What if it's a pizza cow? Then what will you say?"

"MOOO O O O, PIZZA COW!"

"What if it's a pizza snake? Then what will you say?"

SSSSSSSSSS, PIZZA SNAKE!"

"What if it's a pizza dinosaur? Then what will you say?"

"ROAR, PIZZA DINOSAUR!"

RING! RING!

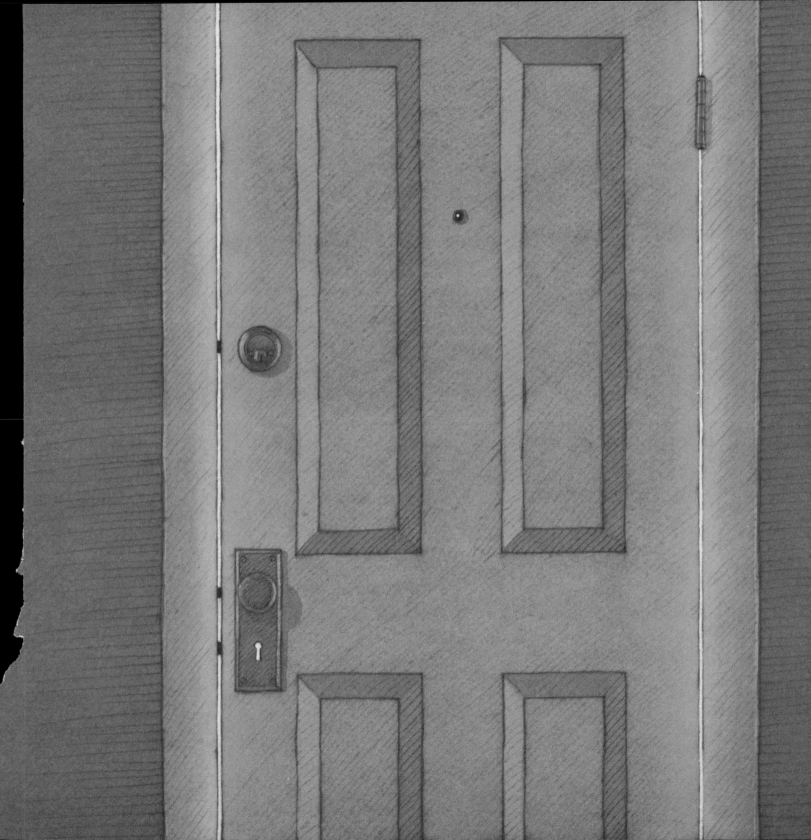

"Hi, Pizza Man!"

To the Mitnick kid

—V.W.

To my daughter, Emma

—P.G.

Copyright © 1995 by Virginia Walter.
Illustrations copyright © 1995 by Ponder Goembel.
All rights reserved. Published by Scholastic Inc., 555 Broadway, New York, NY 10012,
by arrangement with Orchard Books.
SCHOLASTIC and associated logos and designs are trademarks and/or
registered trademarks of Scholastic Inc.

Printed in the U.S.A.

ISBN 0-439-19986-7

4   5   6   7   8   9   10   08   08   07   06   05   04   03   02   01

The text of this book is set in 16 pt. Futura Medium.
The illustrations are ink line and acrylic wash reproduced in full color.